The Mess Detectives
Case #683:
The Trouble with Larry

Written by Doug Peterson
Illustrated by Ron Eddy and Robert Vann

BIG IDEA
BOOKS

zonderkidz

www.bigidea.com

www.zonderkidz.com

The Mess Detectives: Case #683 The Trouble with Larry
Copyright © 2005 by Big Idea, Inc.
Illustrations © 2005 by Big Idea, Inc.

Requests for information should be addressed to:
Grand Rapids, Michigan 49530

Written by: Doug Peterson
Edited by: Amy DeVries, Karen Poth
Illustration and Design: Robert Vann, Ron Eddy
Art Direction: John Trent

Printed in China

05 06 07 08 09 /LPC/ 10 9 8 7 6 5 4 3 2 1

"Let wise people listen and add
to what they have learned."
(Proverbs 1:5)

Ladies and gentlemen, the story you are about to read is silly. The names have been changed to protect the serious.

In the city of Bumblyburg, the worst messes are taken care of by the Major Mess Division. That includes me and my partner.

My name is Detective Larry the
Cucumber, and my partner is Bob the Tomato.
He carries a badge. I carry a badger.

Don't ask why.

We are the Mess Detectives, and this is our story.

9:33 a.m.

I was doodling in my notebook
when an important call came in. Junior
Asparagus was in a big mess at home. We hopped
into our car and sped through town.

As I drove through the streets, Bob tried to tell me
how to get to Junior's house. But I wasn't really listening.
I knew the way.

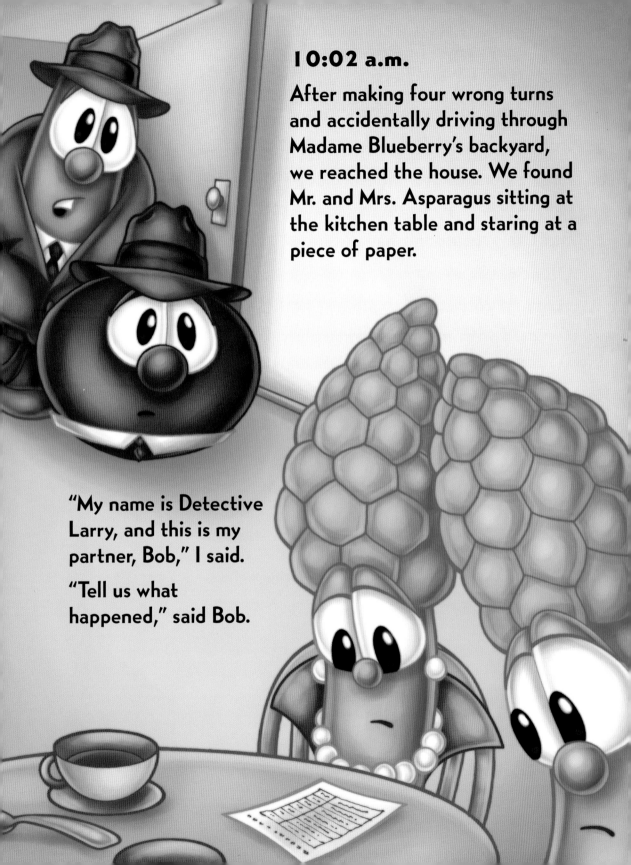

10:02 a.m.

After making four wrong turns and accidentally driving through Madame Blueberry's backyard, we reached the house. We found Mr. and Mrs. Asparagus sitting at the kitchen table and staring at a piece of paper.

"My name is Detective Larry, and this is my partner, Bob," I said.

"Tell us what happened," said Bob.

"It's Junior's report card," said Mr. Asparagus. "He got a bad report from his teachers."

I pulled out some rubber gloves.

"Rubber gloves?" Bob asked.

"I don't want to get fingerprints on the evidence—er, the report card," I said.

"But Larry, you don't have fingers!"

"Oh. Right."

My badger took the gloves. I took a look at the report card with my magnifying glass. "Hmm, doesn't look so bad to me. Junior got an n for 'nice job' in all of his classes."

Bob flipped the report card over. Now, all of the n's looked like u's.

REPORT CARD

U | MATH
CIENCE
ELLING
LISH
CATION
STUDIES

"Yipes!" I said. "I guess Junior got u's for 'unsatisfactory'."

"That means Junior's teachers are unhappy with his schoolwork," explained Bob.

"But why? Why?" asked Mrs. Asparagus.

"We'll find out, ma'am."

As we got ready to leave, I slipped the report card into a plastic bag. That's what detectives do with evidence.

"Uh, Larry," said Bob.

"Yes, Bob."

"You just put the report card in your lunch bag with your tuna-and-peanut-butter sandwich."

10:47 a.m.

We arrived at Veggie Valley Elementary School and set up a two-way mirror in the janitor's closet. We could see Junior's class, but they couldn't see us. Pretty nifty.

While Bob watched Junior, I decided to eat my lunch early. I needed to empty the plastic bags in case we got more evidence.

11:32 a.m.

"Aha! I've figured out why Junior is not doing well in school," Bob said. "He's not listening in class."

"You talking to me?" I asked Bob.

"I said, Junior isn't listening," Bob grumbled. "Just look at him. He's doodling, whispering to other kids, and messing around."

While Bob continued to talk, I cut the crust off my sandwich.

"It's really important to listen, because sometimes God teaches us through the things people say," Bob pointed out. "When you listen, you learn. Don't you agree, Larry? Larry? Larry!"

Startled, I looked up from my sandwich. "Sorry. I wasn't listening."

Bob rolled his eyes. He does that a lot.

1:00 p.m.

We decided to talk with Junior and his parents that evening.

"I'll meet you at Junior's home at six o'clock," Bob told me. He gave me directions to the house. I should have made a note of that. But I wasn't listening.

5:45 p.m.

I hopped in the car to head to Junior's house. But I must have made a wrong turn somewhere. I didn't remember Bob saying anything about driving through Mr. Lunt's petunias.

I was on the highway heading away from Bumblyburg. This couldn't be right. I decided I better call Bob on the car radio.

Only one big problem: I didn't know how to use the new police radio in our car. I wasn't listening when Bob told me.

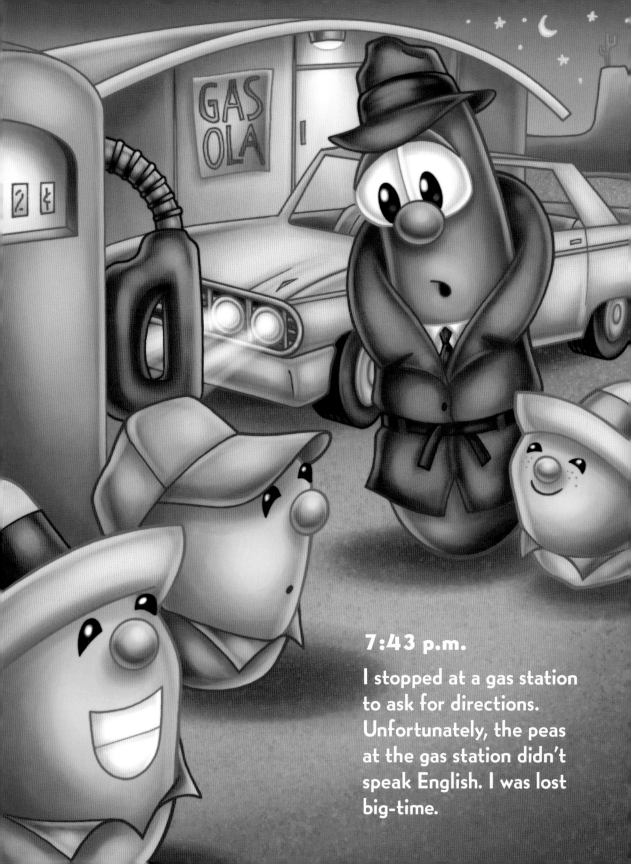

7:43 p.m.

I stopped at a gas station to ask for directions. Unfortunately, the peas at the gas station didn't speak English. I was lost big-time.

8:22 p.m.

Finally, my badger figured out how to use the police radio.

"Bob, come in! Bob, are you there?" said Larry.

"Car 54, where are you?" Bob asked. "Everyone is waiting for you."

"Uh, Bob, I think I'm lost. Your directions didn't say anything about driving by a bull-tickling ring, did they?"

"Bull-tickling?" Bob exclaimed. "Larry, I think you're in Mexico!"

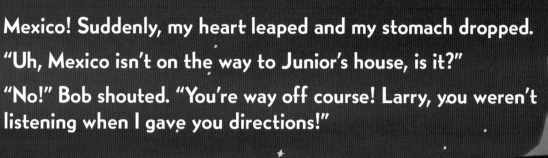

Mexico! Suddenly, my heart leaped and my stomach dropped.

"Uh, Mexico isn't on the way to Junior's house, is it?"

"No!" Bob shouted. "You're way off course! Larry, you weren't listening when I gave you directions!"

Bob was really mad. He was probably turning red in the face.

"Don't you remember what I said?" Bob cried. "When you listen, you learn. Larry! Larry, are you still there?"

Midnight.

Finally, I made it to Junior's house. Mr. Asparagus answered the door in his bathrobe.

"Sorry I'm late, Mr. Asparagus. Are you ready to talk about Junior's problems in school?"

Mr. Asparagus yawned.
"Detective Larry, Bob left a
long time ago.
However, we
do have some
good news."

"I learned
why it's important to
listen," came a voice from the
staircase. It was Junior. "I learned that if you don't listen, you
can wind up in a big mess—just like you, Detective Larry."

"That's right," added Mr. Asparagus. "All evening we listened
to Bob talk to you on the radio. Junior learned that letting his
mind wander in school is a lot like wandering all over the map.
When you don't listen, it can really mess you up."

"Right-O!" I said.

"Also, listening shows you care," said Mr. Asparagus. "If you listen to a teacher or a parent or a friend, it shows you care about them. You care about what they have to say."

I made a note of that.

Suddenly I realized that I too had acted like I didn't care. If I had really cared about Bob, I would have listened to what he had to say.

"Thanks for showing me why I should learn to listen," Junior said to me with a smile.

"Glad to help," I answered. I felt bad about how I had messed up today. "Adios," I said as I went back to my car.

"Adios, Detective Larry!"

1:15 a.m.

I couldn't sleep, so I drove over to Bob's house and asked if we could get a slushie at the All-Night Diner.

"Sorry I didn't listen to you today," I said to Bob.

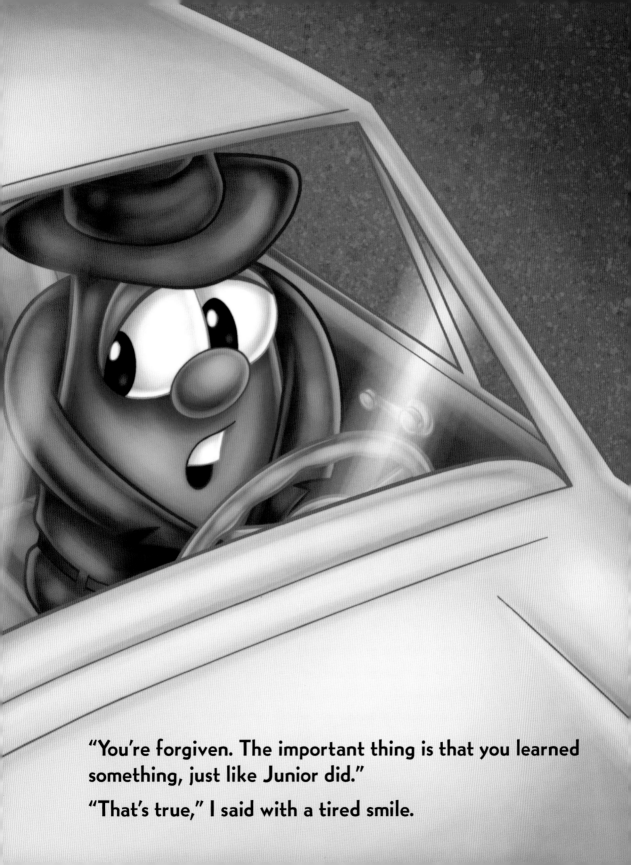

"You're forgiven. The important thing is that you learned something, just like Junior did."

"That's true," I said with a tired smile.

"Maybe this was God's way of teaching you an important lesson," Bob continued. "From now on, you'll listen to what God is trying to say to you."

"You're SOOOO right,"
I said as I made a left
turn.
"Uh, Larry."
"Yes, Bob."

"I don't think you're
supposed to be driving
across Mr. Nezzer's front porch."

"You have a point there," I said, backing the
car down the steps.

Bob gave me directions once again,
but this time I listened.

At long last, I was headed in the right direction.